To Wilson, my home.

To Elena, Florencio and Liliana.

• Lorena Alvarez •

Nightlights

NoBrow

London | New York

Sandy! Go to bed!

Sandy, stop goofing around. You have a big day tomorrow.
I'm a heavy, heavy rock...

Ughh... it's just school.
Come on, up to bed.
Dad, are you going away tomorrow?
Yes, for a big wedding. I won't be gone long.

You finished your homework, didn't you?
Yeah...

And you've polished your shoes?
Yes, mother.

Great! Have a good night, cricket!
Night!

Get up, Sandy!

MOON STREET
BREAKFAST ★ CAFE
HOT TEA

Where's the rest of that skirt, Miss Garcia? This is a sanctuary for learning, not a disco.
Miss Lopez, are you trying to blind me with that pink hairband?
You there! Pull those socks up!

And I don't want to see you wandering off at break again, Sandy.

1.
2.
3.
4.
5.

Hello!
Hi...
Oh, sorry!
I didn't hear you.
Your drawings...
can I see them?

Ok... but they're just doodles.

Are you going to Bible study? We can share mine if you didn't bring yours.
Thanks, but I'm in a different class.

Oh, ok... see you later.

Bye, Sandy.

How...?

...when temptation is upon us, we should run to the side of our Mother in Heaven, cause of our joy...
Hey, Asu.
What?

Have you seen the new girl, Morfie?
Morfie?

What kind of name is that?

Come on! She's tall and pale and her hair is purple.
A weirdo, for sure.

She's not! She said she liked my drawings.
Maybe you saw the girl from the fountain. She drowned there, you know?

Ugh! Stop saying that, Katie.
But I saw her when I fainted during PE!

Stop it!
You're creeping me out!
I'm not lying, Asu!
ENOUGH!
You think our Blessed Mother doesn't deserve your attention, miss?
Ha ha! Busted!

You won't go far in life looking out of the window.

And… is that a cookie, Asu? Put that away, we just had lunch!

RIIIIIIIIIIIIIIIINNNG!!!

God bless you girls, and have a good evening!

White Illusions
GAMMA PRINTS
•COLOR •INTERNET •FAX •COPIES
WORKOUT! 333124
THE SUNFLOWER
•BAKERY•
POSH
FASHION
NEW DESIGNS EVERIDAY
SALE!!!
DELIVER

Hey, Sandy!
?

Let's walk home together. How was school today?
I met the new girl, and we're already friends!

She's so nice! Her name is Morfie and she likes my drawings! I'm going to draw something for her tonight.

Don't you have homework to do first?
Humph! Yeah...

Good evening!
Hello, Nicky!

Take your books and go upstairs. I'll bring you a snack to help you concentrate.
Ok

I'm so happy you made a new friend, San.

Hello
Who's there?

I love your drawings...
You make things out
of thin air.

Can you show
me how you do it?
Oh, it's not that hard.
I catch the lights and they turn into
anything I can imagine. Then I draw
them so they stay with me!

What is that?
How did I make that?
Aw...
it's cute!

No! Something
strange is happening.
Draw for me, Sandy,
and I'll make the
lights reappear.

Why? I've never
needed you before!
Ah... but you will!

I admire you so much!
And once you realize that you need me to tell you...
...how brilliant you are...

...nothing will keep us apart!
Don't worry, Sandy. You'll change your mind...

Come on, Sandy.
It's getting late!

You want some hot chocolate, Sandy?

Or maybe some orange juice?
Cricket, are you ok? You look like you've barely slept! We can take the bus together if you want?
I'm fine.

* Pronounced /pai /

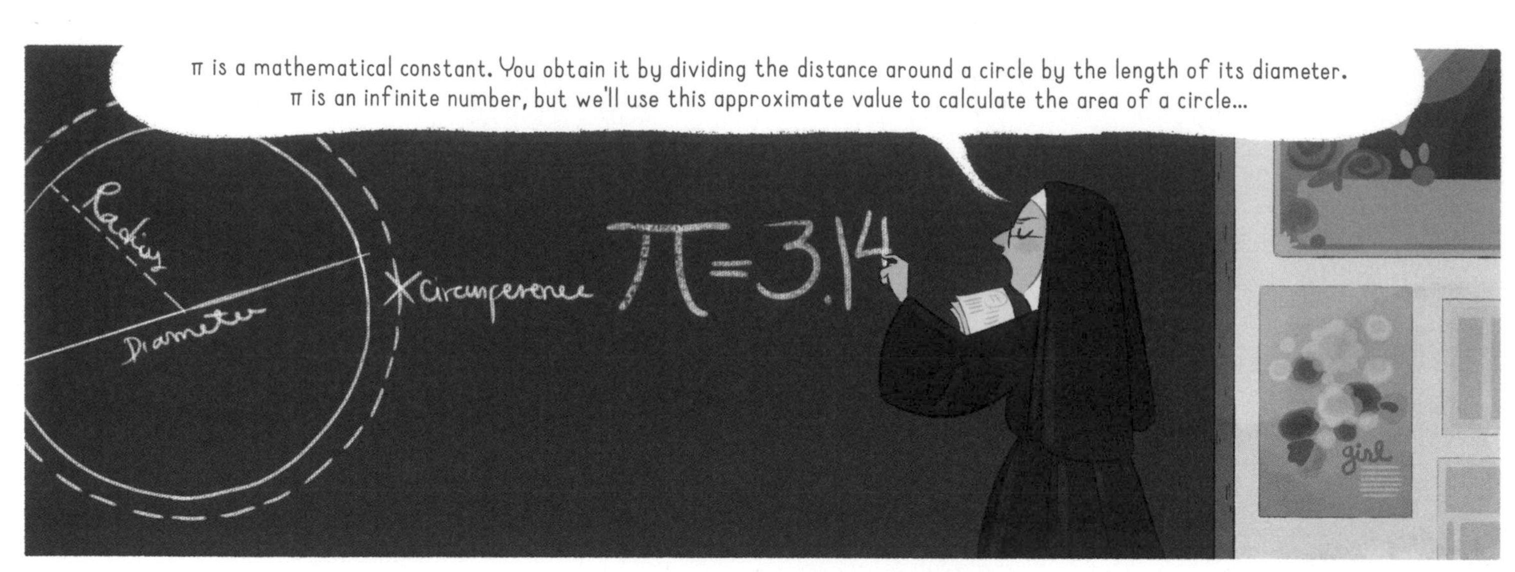
π is a mathematical constant. You obtain it by dividing the distance around a circle by the length of its diameter.
π is an infinite number, but we'll use this approximate value to calculate the area of a circle...
Radius
Diameter
Circumference
π=3.14

...with the help of one of you girls ...Sandy?

Sandy??

SANDY!

Could you stop daydreaming and write out the equation?
Beep! Earth calling Sandy!
Beep!

And the spaceship goes up!
Ha ha!

And up...
She's so weird.

And... kaboom!
What a doofus!

Show me your notebook, Sandy.
circumference
π=3.1459....
π=

HUMPH!

You think these doodles are more important than this class?

Don't waste my time with your nonsense. If you're not going to pay attention, you can sit somewhere else.

You will stay here, while the other girls are using their minds for something useful.

Now sit down and write 300 times: I won't waste my time drawing in class.

And don't touch anything!

!!!

Hey,
Sandy!
My biology teacher sent
me to get this ugly bug.
Don't do that!
This place is creepy!

Are you in trouble?
I can totally help you,
I write really fast.

See? 300 lines.
Done!
Already?
And they look even!

Class is so boring!
Let's stay here.

We've been waiting for you, most powerful sorceress!

After this long journey I finally have the power to talk to animals and make trees grow on my command.

And now the hardest part of the surgery: to put the brain where the heart used to be...

Here comes the moon!

I bet there's a lot of these ugly things crawling around the school grounds.
I really do like your drawings, Sandy.
A girl's praye

Yes, Sister,
I understand...

No, please
don't worry.
I'll talk to her...

Sandy? Are you there?

I know... Yes, Sister.
Have a good evening...
You too...

SISTER DOLORE

Are you going to tell me what happened in class?

I got in trouble with Sister Dolores. I had to write lines...

Ok, I know Sister Dolores is quite scary, but you should stay focused in class.
I know...

Even if you don't like it...
It's not that!

Then tell me what it is!
I don't know!

Sandy!

TOC!

Morfie?

How did you get here?
I just climbed up!

It's not that hard. You should come with me. There's a place I want to show you.
That's a very tall tree...

Don't be silly! Come on!
Wait! I don't want my sweater to get caught.

Hey! Don't look up!
Ha ha! They're blue.

I forgot to pin my skirt.

Told you it wasn't hard.

How far are we going?
Don't worry, Sandy, you're going to love this place.
It's really dark... where are we?
Shhhh, this is the perfect spot!

Nobody will ever bother us here! Just imagine all the things you can draw.

Here! I brought your notebook.

Morfie... When did you take my things?
I can already feel all the things you will draw for me.

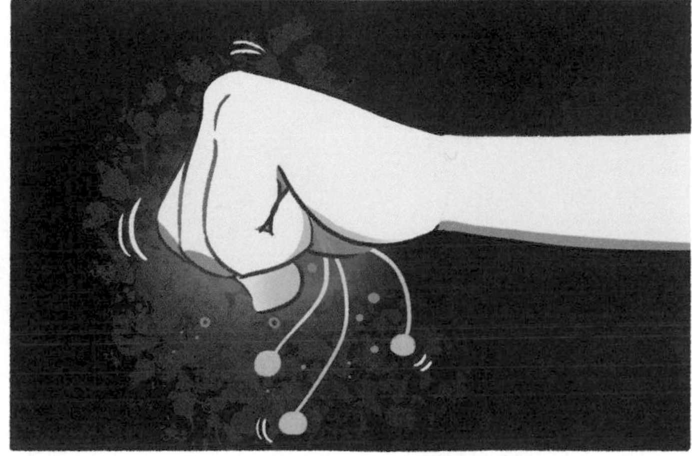

M...Morfie?

Hello

Have you thought about our little chat?
Go away! I don't need you!

But, Sandy, just imagine...

...a perfect place just for you.

You will stay with us...
...and draw for us, and we will feed upon your drawings. You will make us happy and we will love you forever.

We will never leave you...

...won't it be wonderful?

I...

Isn't this what you want?

Because I do!

You do need us, Sandy.
You'll never be able to draw again if you don't feed us!

And you know we're stronger than you!
Let me go!

Don't hurt me!
I'll stay with you!!

Perfect!

But if you really want my drawings...

...you have to do something for me first.

I can't draw until I've done my homework...

Sister Dolores asked me to write all the digits of π. You know how scary she is...
Sure!

...and you wrote those 300 lines so fast the last time! I'm sure you won't have any problem with a few numbers.
I won't. I can help you!

3.14159...

2653589...

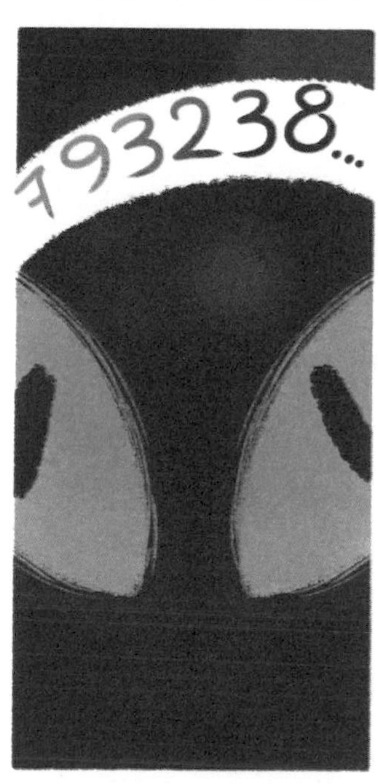
793238...

462643...

8419716939937510582097494459230...

Hi

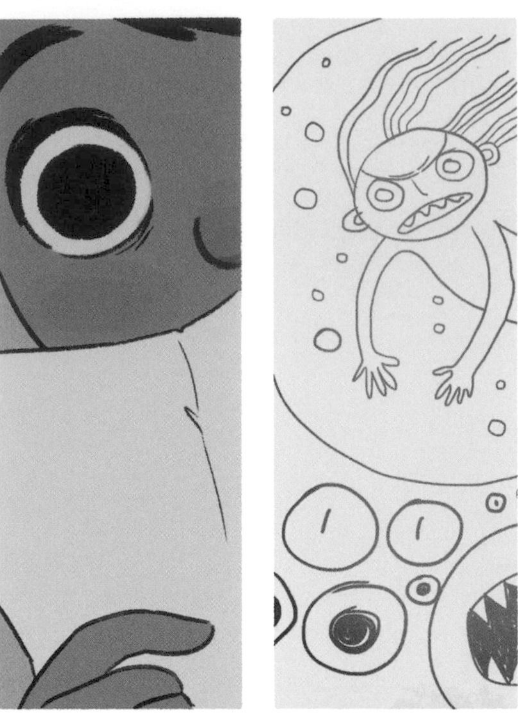

Sandy, you're late!

Look at that hair! No doubt Sister Dolores will have something to say about it.

Bye!

Go to the nurse and clean off that blue nail polish now!

GOOD MOOoRNING SISTER PIEDAAAAD!!!

Good morning girls, a new lesson awaits us today.

Atoms are the smallest building blocks of matter.

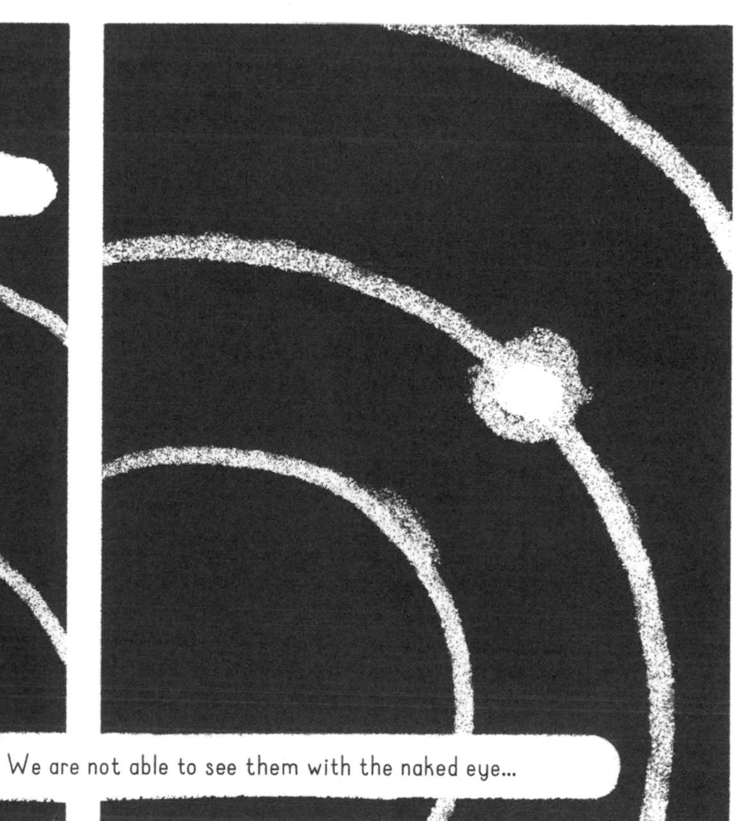
We are not able to see them with the naked eye...

...but everything that surrounds us is made of atoms.
The stars...
...our bodies...
...the entire universe.

They combine in millions
of ways to create all the
things we see and touch...

...and the things we haven't seen yet.

This is a third edition. First published in 2016
by Nobrow Ltd. 27 Westgate Street, London E8 3RL.

Published in the US by Nobrow (US) Inc.
Printed in Poland on FSC® certified paper.

ISBN: 978-1-910620-13-7

Order from www.nobrow.net

• Lorena Alvarez •

Born and raised in Bogotá, Colombia, Lorena's work is influenced by the vibrancy and colour of her home town as well as the experiences and atmosphere of the Catholic school she attended as a child.

She studied Graphic Design and Arts at the Universidad Nacional de Colombia, and has since illustrated for children's books, independent publications, advertising and fashion magazines.

Since 2008, Lorena has been part of "La Procesión Puppet Club", an experimental puppetry group of illustrators and visual artists.